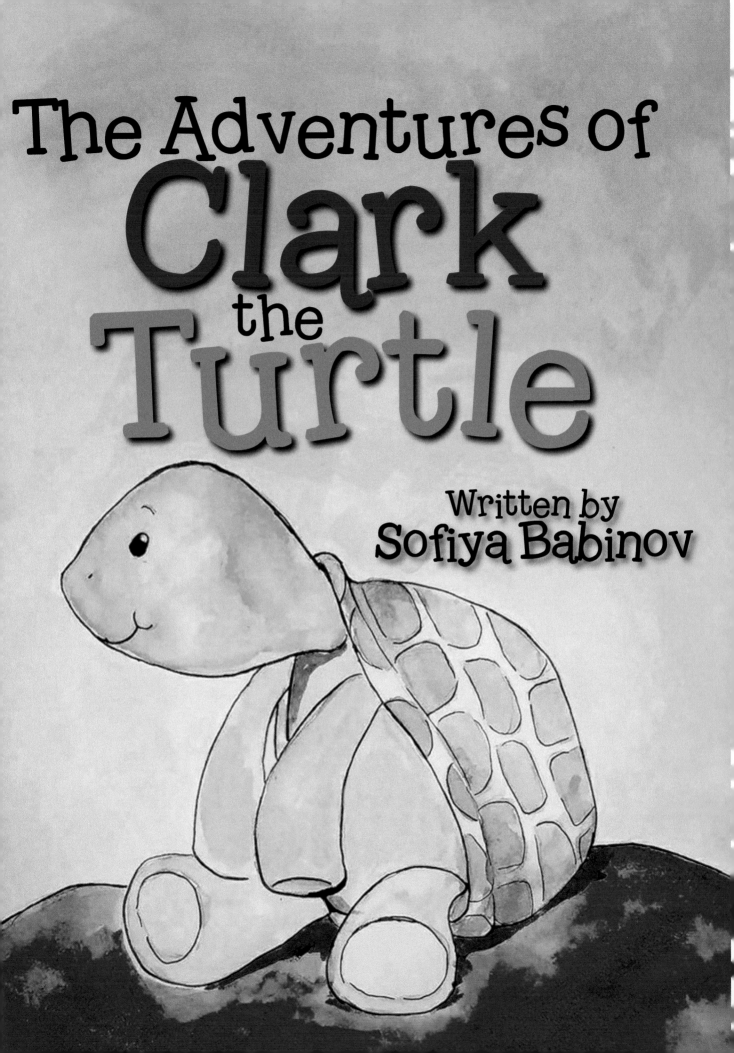

Print information available on the last page

Rev. date: 03/19/2018

To order additional copies of this book, contact:
Xlibris
1-888-795-4274
www.Xlibris.com
Orders@Xlibris.com

The Adventures of Clark the Turtle

Hi! My name is Abel, and I'm a five-year-old boy.
Let me tell you about my favorite toy!

I have a stuffed animal turtle, and his name is Clark.
He goes with me on all my adventures, from morning until dark.

I bought him at a store one day.
And he's my best friend, even today!

My parents think that Clark's a toy.
But he is just like me, a boy!

He talks and listens. He even gives me advice
on how to share, behave my best, and be nice.

I can't go anywhere without my Clark.
His favorite place to go is the park.

He likes the swing, the monkey bars, and the slide.
The slide is Clark boy's favorite ride!

We always find ways to have fun,
if only Clark knew how to run!

We'd play tag on the trampoline
and hide until we can't be seen.

Mommy said it's time for dinner.
Whoever eats first will be the
winner!

I eat healthy food to grow strong and tall.
Vegetables and fruits, I eat them all.

To end the day, it's bath-time fun.

I get so sweaty when I run!

Clark takes baths in the washing machine.
He comes out smelling fresh and clean!

At bedtime, we're tucked in for the night.
I turn on my night-light and hug Clark tight!

It's been a great day for my best friend and me.
I can't wait to see how fun tomorrow will be!

19

Dedication

I would like to dedicate this book to my beloved husband Michael, my precious son Abel, and all my family and friends!

I would like to thank and acknowledge my friend and illustrator Kseniya Wong, and my friend Meredith Kay who were very instrumental in me writing this book.

I would also like to dedicate this book to children all over the world!

A portion of all proceeds from this book will go to help fund international orphanages and other organizations that support orphans.

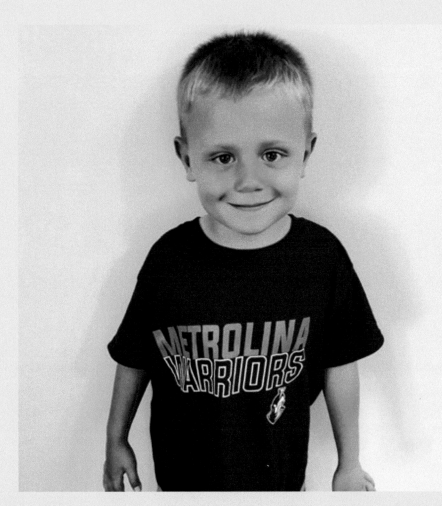

My little co-author and son, Abel Babinov.